About the Author

Zoe has lived in several countries and is fluent in Spanish. She enjoys travelling the world and experiencing different cultures. Also a singer/songwriter, Zoe's creative passion and imagination for writing stories and music were sparked at an early age and continued into adulthood.

Dedication

To my wonderful husband, Simon, and forever friend, Doogs, for your continuous support and for always believing in me.

Zoe C. Barnes

DYING TO KNOW

AUSTIN MACAULEY PUBLISHERS™

LONDON • CAMBRIDGE • NEW YORK • SHARJAH

A CIP catalogue record for this title is available from the British Library.

ISBN 9781528904940 (Paperback)
ISBN 9781528957861 (ePub e-book)

www.austinmacauley.com

First Published (2019)
Austin Macauley Publishers Ltd
25 Canada Square
Canary Wharf
London
E14 5LQ

Acknowledgements

Thank you to my husband, Simon Highton, David Copeland, Sadie, Linda Thompson (drama would not have been the same without you) and to all of those who have inspired me throughout my life.

London, 12th February 1977

She knew, as soon as she opened the front door and stepped into the hallway, that something wasn't right, call it a gut feeling or natural intuition, which would serve her well later in life, Stella just knew. 'Mum!' she called as she went into the kitchen, nothing, no reply. 'Mum!' she called again, this time slightly louder. Still no reply just an eerie silence. Her mother, Marnie, was always at home at this time. Marnie worked as a chef in a very popular, top London restaurant in the West End. She worked very hard but was always at home to greet Stella from school. Stella climbed the stairs and turned left towards her mother's room. The sight that greeted Stella would change her forever, turning a young, innocent 13-year-old girl into the woman she was to become. Lying on her bed, blood dripping from her wrists, was Marnie, eyes wide open, staring up at the ceiling. Stella was so shocked, completely numb, that she can't remember if she screamed, but she must have as, within minutes, the neighbour from the downstairs flat came rushing in. Stella remembered that from that moment, everything appeared to happen in slow motion. Bert, the neighbour ushering her out of the room, Bert calling the police, the police arriving and running up the stairs to their flat, a bearded PC and a pretty, petite, blonde WPC who escorted Stella downstairs and out of the flat into the waiting police car. She remembered the bearded PC coming out of the front door speaking on his walkie-talkie, an intense look on his face. She remembered the ambulance arriving and the two paramedics walking towards the front door, med kits in hand, she remembered the pretty WPC holding her hand, a sad look in her bright blue eyes, 'I'm so sorry, sweetheart, everything's going to be alright,' the kind lady had whispered. The bearded

PC got into the car, and whilst driving away, Stella looked out of the window and started humming a lullaby to herself that her mother used to sing to her when she was very young. Stella's mother was dead. Her beautiful, caring, funny mum whom Stella adored was gone and life for Stella as she knew it ceased to be on that fateful day.

Present day

Stella Sinclair-Matthews had always been an inquisitive, some would go as far as saying extremely nosy, individual. Even throughout her schooldays, she was always putting her nose in where it wasn't wanted, making her popular (for all the latest gossip) and unpopular at the same time for, as some of her classmates had put it, being too overbearing. Stella knew that she changed after her mother died. Something died inside Stella that day also, she couldn't explain it, but emotionally, things felt very different. Before losing her mother, Stella had always been confident and outgoing, but since her tragic loss, she had become harder somehow. In 1986, it had made perfect sense that after working in the legal profession since she had left school, that she become a private investigator and a very successful one at that, offering a "professional and discreet service" to all her clients. She remembered one of her very first cases not long after she had set up her business. It had been for a very respected and established businessman in London. He and his partner ran an import and export company. He was convinced that his business partner was up to no good as money had gone missing. Large amounts of money. Rather than call him out, he had decided to see what Stella could come up with before he called the police and got them involved. He gave her all the information she required, along with a portfolio on his business partner. Low and behold, within two weeks, Stella had not only found him to be embezzling money from the company but also that he had started up a company of his own in Switzerland, which made perfect sense as he was able to transfer the money without anyone asking too many questions. The police were called, and along with all the evidence, his colleague was convicted of fraud and spent time in prison. Her client was very impressed and through that one job, Stella's reputation as a very thorough and tough investigator grew as did her bank balance she was pleased to see. Stella met many, wealthy and important people through her line of work and got to rub shoulders with a few celebrities along the way, as well as politicians and the like. She was invited to parties at beautiful mansions and, at times, had to pinch herself at how far she'd come, and for that, she was incredibly proud of herself.

London, March 1977

It had been just over a month since Stella had arrived home to find her beautiful mother, Marnie, dead. Suicide, slashed her wrists, took her own life. She was gone, gone forever. It had been Marnie's wishes that her sister Gabby become Stella's legal guardian. They had always been close, and there was no question as to who would bring Stella up. Stella had never known her father. He had disappeared long before Stella was born. 'What was he like, Mum?' Stella had asked her mum when she was about eight years old.

'Stells (this was Marnie's nickname for Stella), we only went out a few times. I met him at the restaurant. He used to come in with his colleagues at lunchtime and have a few drinks. He complimented me on my cooking, and we went out a few times. He was fun to be with, made me laugh but I knew it wasn't really going anywhere.' Stella wanted to know more but there wasn't much more to tell. 'I fell pregnant with you, and when I told him, I thought he had a right to know, he didn't know what to say. He seemed scared and completely disinterested. I knew in that moment that he wasn't dad material; after that, I didn't hear from him. I was so happy and excited to be pregnant, and Gabby was all the support I needed.' Marnie and Gabby had always been incredibly close growing up and Stella adored her Aunt Gabby. She was like a second mum to her. At the funeral, Stella placed a single red rose on her mother's coffin, and as it was being lowered into the ground, she remembered thinking that the rose would soon be dead, along with her mother. Life was horrible, unfair. Why did this have to happen to her, why?

'Stella, sweetheart,' Gabby interrupted her thoughts.

'Yes, Aunt Gabby.'

'I've been thinking, we should go to the summer house in Cornwall next weekend, the fresh sea air would do you the world of good and I could do with a break too, work has been horrendously busy lately and I'm exhausted.'

'Great, I'd really enjoy that,' Stella replied. She had been to her aunt's summer house a few times in her life and it was such a pretty place. Gabby called it the summerhouse, but she went there throughout the year when she felt stressed, needed a break or just wanted to enjoy the fresh air and leave the hectic London life behind once in a while. Stella and Marnie would run on the beach, swim in the sea, laugh and play. They were good times, wonderful memories. They say that you are unable to remember anything as a baby, but Stella vividly remembered being about two years old, walking along the sea's edge, the cold water splashing at her tiny feet, giggling as though she would burst as her mother took her tiny hands and lifted her up towards the summer sun. She can even remember the breeze as it blew her beautiful mother's hair across her face. She felt such love. But, was it a memory or a yearning to hold her mother close just one more time and to tell her how much she loved and missed her? Gabby had a very good job in the city as a financial whiz. She had left school with hardly any qualifications but had put herself through night school and trained as an accountant and an excellent one at that, which then led to her being headhunted for bigger and better things. She had done very well for herself, and apart from having her spacious one bedroom flat in London, she owned the house by the sea in Cornwall. Gabby and Marnie were so close, and Stella knew that she too was heartbroken at losing her only sister. Stella had never known her grandparents. They'd passed away when Marnie and Gabby were in their 20s. She'd catch Gabby looking at old photographs of when they were young and carefree, a look of sadness in her eyes. Stella knew she was trying to stay strong for her sake and she loved her aunt dearly. It was her and Aunt Gabby facing the world together, holding onto their grief like a safety blanket and each suffering alone, each not wanting to upset the other.

Present day

Her husband, Roger, was the complete opposite to Stella, rather shy, lacking in confidence and dare she say it, at times, quite boring. She didn't mean this in a nasty way but since they had met, Roger had changed slightly. Or had she changed? The thing that first attracted her to Roger was his kind nature and his smile. He had the most mesmerising smile that could light up a room. They had dated for just over a year when Roger had asked Stella to marry him. 'You know how much I love you, don't you?' he had asked her as they were eating dinner one evening at their favourite Italian restaurant near the beach in Cornwall. She had blushed for some reason. She wasn't really into public displays of affection. 'Of course, I do,' she had replied, yet for some reason, she didn't tell him she loved him back. It wasn't that she didn't love him, but because she just couldn't find the words. 'Stella, will you be my wife?' he was down on one knee and the whole restaurant had turned around to look at him. 'Oh Roger, I don't know what to say!'

'Yes, would be nice' Roger replied, searching Stella's face for an answer.

'Yes, I will, of course, I will,' replied Stella. The surrounding tables and the waiters erupted into applause. He kissed her on the lips and hugged her close. 'Thank you for making me the happiest man alive, Stella Matthews.' Yes, Roger adored Stella, worshipped the ground she walked on, and they had been married for almost ten years. Roger's life had been completely different to Stella's. He came from a loving, if somewhat regimented family background. His father was in the army and he had travelled the world with him, his mother and brother since he was young. He had lived in Singapore, India, Germany and many other interesting countries. Stella often wondered if that was why he was so different from her. His father had been very strict, and she felt that Roger was shy and introvert as a result of this kind of upbringing. They were nice people, however. After his father retired from the army, they moved to Spain and bought an old farmhouse in a small town in the southeast. They had restored it to its natural beauty, and it was a stunning house. It was a beautiful place to live and they were very content over there. Roger, much to his father's discontent had no desire to follow in his footsteps. After studying horticulture at university, he had started his own landscaping business and a successful one at that. When he wasn't working, he was content spending most of the time in their immaculate garden, planting flowers, pulling weeds, trimming hedges, visiting their local garden centre where he would spend hours choosing plants, seeds, garden ornaments and the latest "must have" garden tool. So, while Stella delved into other peoples' lives only to deliver, more often than not, bad and upsetting news, due to her findings, Roger was happily content in his life doing what he also loved. Most of her cases nowadays involved finding out what a spouse or partner was up to and, more often than not, infidelity was the outcome. She remembered one of her latest cases. It involved a doctor, a neurosurgeon. She'd been married to her husband of 15 years, a geologist. 'He and I have not been seeing eye to eye lately, I don't know, he seems distant yet at the same time, like he's always been, if that makes sense,' she had told Stella when they had met at her immaculate home set in acres of land. 'Okay, he travels a lot, I'm constantly working, I get home late from the hospital, but when we are together, it's like we're strangers. I mean I know that many couples have work commitments, travel with work, but I don't know, he just ignores me when I try and bring the subject up about us, about what's happened to us, even our daughters have noticed, they're 14 and 12.'

'What is your gut feeling?' Stella had asked her.

'He has been away a lot this year, with his job, but I just get the feeling there's something wrong, something he's not telling me,' her client had replied. Two hours later, Stella was driving home armed with a file on her client's husband, photos, his background, his routine. Everything Stella requested in order to get to work. She was to call her client as soon as there was any news. 'Anything, however silly or out of the ordinary,' her client had said, 'call me immediately.'

'Of course, no problem,' Stella had replied. She didn't need telling. Less than a month later, Stella had uncovered more than an affair, and for the first time in her career, she actually dreaded telling her client her news. Not only was there someone else, but the woman in question had been a part of his life for over five years and was the mother to two of his children. As Stella drove to meet her client, she felt very uneasy. 'Oh my God, oh my God,' her client had whispered when Stella placed all the evidence in front of her, photos of them together, along with their children, a boy and a girl, of him leaving her house, walking together along the beach hand in hand, sharing a kiss.

'I'm so sorry,' Stella said gently as she watched the tears stream down her client's face. To uncover an affair is one thing, but to uncover another life was something else. Yes, that case had left Stella feeling particularly low. 'Stella, love, what are your plans for today?' asked Roger over breakfast, that rainy and dull Monday morning.

'I'm working Roger' she replied, maybe a little too harshly. She had received a phone call from a man called Steven Abbott and he seemed very keen to meet with her as soon as possible. 'No problem, darling, it's just that I thought we could do something today, a meal, film or something.'

Ah, poor Roger, I really should make more time for us as a couple, thought Stella. They got on very well and were close, despite being very different. 'Maybe at the weekend, Roger, maybe at the weekend,' she replied, not really convincing as she was now getting her things together to meet Steve at a café in town. They used to do a lot together, even when they were busy working, they'd always catch a film, eat out a few times a week or spend cosy nights in, nowadays, it was like there wasn't enough time in the day. She was always busy, he was always busy, but, and she hated to admit it, Roger did try and make more of an effort than her, trying to arrange days out or weekend away. 'We'll definitely do something soon, Roger, okay,' she shouted as she picked up her keys.

'Yes, darling, of course, no worries,' Roger replied, as understanding as ever. Within minutes, she was out of the front door and in her car, quite intrigued and excited at the prospect of meeting another client who required her help. She should really slow down though, she had been feeling tired of late, rushing around all the time, getting out of breath and not getting enough sleep. A few years earlier, she had started to suffer panic attacks after a particularly horrible and draining case that had sapped her of her energy. It was not like her, she was strong, didn't suffer from stress, or maybe just dealt with it better than most, but it hadn't concerned her enough to go to the doctor, despite Roger's nagging insisting, she went and saw him. After a couple of weeks, the panic attacks disappeared as quickly as they had started. Maybe a nice holiday is what they needed, a chance to reconnect and recharge their batteries. They could back to the place they had honeymooned, Thailand. It really was a beautiful place and incredibly peaceful. She thought back to that time. They had arrived in Bangkok to the hustle and bustle and intense humidity. It was such a manic city yet rather calming at the same time. They had visited the Royal Palace and most of the temples. Their favourite was the Golden Buddha. They'd walked around the grounds for ages, holding hands, shielding themselves from the blazing sun under an umbrella they bought from a street vendor for 100 Bhat. 'You buy, madam, very cheap, very good,' the young man had said. Stella remembered strolling through a street market on the Koh San Road and they'd come across a stall selling deep-fried insects. Before she knew it, Roger, introvert and shy Roger, had put a dead locust in his mouth and was chewing away! She was so shocked that her husband would do this that she had grabbed the camera from her bag and taken a photo as evidence. His face was a picture and they'd laughed and laughed. The remainder of their honeymoon had been spent in Koh Samui. As a surprise, Roger had booked one of the most expensive hotels on the island with its own private beach. Their honeymoon suite was magnificent. Stella had never seen anything quite like it, despite having stayed in five-star luxurious hotels many times before. The room had a huge balcony that looked straight onto the beach and the blue ocean beneath. There were majestic palm trees outside their balcony which looked at least 100 years old, and you could hear the swish of the breeze flow through the leaves. They'd enjoyed heavenly massages together in the privacy of their room. She could still remember the gorgeous, relaxing smell of the oils, lemongrass and bamboo. They'd made love almost every night and enjoyed every minute of every day. Yes, that was a happy time and maybe just what she and Roger both needed. They were still quite affectionate when they were together, held hands, cuddled on the sofa but she did feel their love life had been neglected of late. She, although she didn't like to admit this, knew it was mostly down to her. She wasn't great with words, never had been, but Roger was so understanding, as always. There was no doubt about it. Some quality time together would be good for them both. 'Bye, Roger, see you later, have a good day.'

'Bye, darling, you too,' Roger replied. She gave a wry smile, opened the front door, got into her car and drove away from the house.

London, July 1984

Soon after her 20th birthday, Stella had moved out of her aunt's comfy flat and rented a flat in Battersea with her friend, Beth. 'You know I'm here for you whenever you need me, don't you, sweetheart?' Gabby had told her as she was packing her belongings into her old banger, a car she had owned for a couple of years. 'Yes, I know you are, Aunt Gabby, and you have no idea how much that means to me, I'm going to miss you so much!' She had never called her "Gabby". It had always been Aunt Gabby. Her aunt had offered to buy her a new car, but Stella wouldn't hear of it. 'I love my little car and it's perfect for city life,' she had told Gabby. Stella had always had an independent streak, some would say hard, but she didn't want it any other way. 'Here, here's a little flat warming present,' Gabby said as she placed a brown envelope in her hand. 'Go on, open it!' Gabby said. Stella put her bag down and opened the envelope. Inside was a cheque for £2,000. 'Aunt Gabby, I can't take this!' Stella had cried.

'You can and you will,' Gabby replied with determination in her voice. 'I know that apart from being this beautiful, intelligent and young woman, that you're very independent and you don't like taking anything from me, but let's not forget that I've seen the furniture in this new place of yours and to say it's awful is an understatement!' She had a point though. It was old, grubby and belonged in the 60s. 'Aw, you're the best aunt anyone could wish for,' Stella replied, reaching over and giving her aunt a big hug. Stella had managed to save some money, but this would really come in handy and help make the flat cosy and a nice place to live for her and Beth. Stella had studied hard at school and had a job as a secretary in a law firm. She loved her job and it gave her a thrill. Typing up manuscripts for different cases, taking notes at important meetings and reading through files had left her buzzing after a long day. Her bosses were quite impressed with her hard work and determination. Beth and Stella had been best friends at school and shared a lot of common interests like travelling, local markets, eating out, going to the cinema and the odd bottle of wine although it was safe to say that Beth was the bigger drinker of the two, often waking up with a raging hangover and a mood to go with it. Beth hadn't enjoyed school as much as Stella and she had a job working in a clothes shop on Oxford Street. Beth thought of herself as a bit of a fashionista. Also, Stella was dating Beth's brother, Jason. They'd been dating for just over a year and she could not have been happier. Due to his work, she didn't see much of him, at least not as much as she would have liked. He was policeman and four years older than her and Beth. Jason was strong, handsome, outgoing and a bit of a jack the lad, but Stella had fallen hard, and he did treat her well even if he did prefer going out with his mates rather than her lately. She was very mature for 20, and despite the trauma of losing her mother, very serious, to the point and fair. She believed that life was too short to not say what you're thinking. Jason was her first serious boyfriend. She'd had the odd fling but, this time, she felt different. Beth was always teasing her, 'Shall I buy a hat yet?' she had joked. She had always thought Jason was cute and funny, even when she'd stay over at Beth's house after school and their mum would make the best fish finger sandwiches ever! Jason was very popular at school. He was brainy too. She remembered trying to flirt with him, but he never really noticed her back then. To him, she was probably just a silly, young girl and, while she'd listened to all the latest and cutest boy bands, Jason was more into rock bands. Stella often wondered what her mum would have thought of him. She was sure she would have loved him as much as she did. In fact, Stella found herself thinking about how her life would have been different had she had still been alive. Would they have stayed in the same flat, would her mum still be working as a chef, would she have met someone that made her happy and accepted Stella as his own? She would never know. 'Come here, you gorgeous,' Jason said, putting his strong, manly arms around her. 'Why don't we book a hotel next weekend as I'm off and I thought it would do us good; I feel like we haven't spent any quality time together at all lately.'

'Oh, let me see; let me check my diary,' Stella replied, in a teasing voice. 'That sounds absolutely wonderful!' she exclaimed, not wanting him to let her go.

'Oh my God, what are you two like,' Beth teased as she walked into the living room. 'Put her down, please!'

Stella laughed and kissed Jason. He was so sexy, so popular, she was so lucky to be with him. She couldn't wait for the following weekend to arrive. They would spend it together in a romantic hotel, making love, laughing and just being together, bliss, thought Stella, pure bliss. Just thinking about the following weekend filled her with excitement. She couldn't remember the last time she'd been this happy.

Present day

As Stella sat sipping her coffee and watching the pouring rain through the window, she noticed the tall, dark, athletic man get out of his car and run towards the café. As he came through the door, already wet from the rain, he glanced over at Stella and she smiled. 'Hi, you must be Stella?' She shook his hand, 'Nice to meet you, Mr Abbott.'

'Steve, please,' he replied. He ordered a coffee and sat down opposite Stella. He seemed rather nervous, shy almost, as though he shouldn't really be there. Stella waited for him to speak first. 'Look, I'm probably, hopefully,' he added nervously, 'wasting your time, but it's my wife, Jodie. Something isn't right.' Stella looked at him sympathetically but still said nothing. 'It's nothing concrete, nothing I can really put my finger on, it's just… he trailed off. He started to look very uncomfortable and Stella sensed it was time to talk. 'What do you think it could be, Steve?' she asked, compassionately.

'Well, it's, and this may sound stupid, it's like she's being too nice.' Stella took a sip of her coffee. 'Look, a couple of years back, we went through a bad patch, all my doing, to do with my business, but we talked it all through and everything was, is, good now, but, I don't know, it's like she is hiding something, shit, I don't know, I feel really embarrassed and stupid.' Steve looked down at his coffee then blurted, a little louder than he had anticipated, 'I think she could be having an affair!'

'Okay,' Stella replied softly. 'Look, Steve, I'm not going to sit here and lie to you, but in my years of experience, I have delivered bad news to my clients regarding their spouse's infidelity, but not always, so please don't imagine the worst, okay?' He handed her a photograph of Jodie along with a detailed account of her weekly routine. She was classically beautiful with long, dark hair and a figure most women would envy. She looked familiar. She looked at Steve, sipping his coffee with such sadness in his handsome face that she really hoped that after following Jodie and putting a file together that he would be wrong, that she could report back that nothing was going on, that Jodie was not having an affair and they could live happily ever after. 'Let's give it a week and we'll meet again with my findings,' Stella said.

'That sounds good,' Steve replied although the look on his face said something different. Steve got up first to leave. 'It was nice to meet you, Stella, and please, if you need to phone me in the meantime, here's my business card.' Stella understood he didn't want her to phone him at home. 'I'll get these,' Steve said and paid for the coffees. 'Thank you and I'll be in touch.' She watched him leave and for some reason, felt sorry for him. She finished her coffee and went on her way. As Steve was driving home, he started to worry that he had done the wrong thing, getting a private investigator involved in what was probably just his paranoia. He felt quite embarrassed and angry that he had met with Stella, but it was done now. He could not live without her, without Jodie in his life. She was his soulmate. The thought of her with anyone else made him feel physically sick. He remembered the first time he had laid eyes on her. She was standing next to the wine rack at their local wine bar. She literally took his breath away. She was the most beautiful woman he had ever seen. She was tall with long, dark hair and olive skin. She turned and saw him looking at her. 'Hi. Hi there, see anything you like?' As soon as the words left his lips, he felt like a complete idiot. She smiled politely and said, 'Yes, I love the Chilean Red, full of oaky flavours, full-bodied, it's my favourite.' An hour later, he found himself sitting with Jodie sharing the bottle of wine she had commented on, along with Spanish olives and cheese, not wanting the evening to end. He was smitten, completely smitten. From that day on, they started dating and became inseparable. She moved in with him only two months later and he was the happiest he had ever been in his life. He thought back to their first holiday together in a little fishing village in Greece. They'd rented a little beach house and would spend their days exploring the island on a moped, taking in the beautiful scenery, eating delicious, local food and tanning their bodies on the sandy beaches. Each night, after passionate lovemaking that lasted for hours, they'd fall asleep in each other's arms and he could not believe just how lucky he was to have met such an amazing, beautiful, sexy woman. He proposed on that very holiday, on a mountain top overlooking the sea below. That seemed like many moons ago now. He was a successful property developer and they enjoyed a great lifestyle. A few years earlier, he had invested in a deal that was to make him a lot of money, but it had not gone according to plan and he had lost hundreds of thousands of pounds. He hadn't told Jodie. Call it male pride and the fact that he had other deals going through and was going to put the money back and she would never have found out had she not gone to the bank, to their joint account. 'What the hell is this?' she had screamed waving a bank statement in his face that Friday evening as he walked through the door. 'Babe, calm down, please, I can explain.'

'Calm down, calm down, start talking now!' she was screaming, her face contorted with rage. He had never, ever seen his wife this angry before and he was taken off guard, her rage scared him. 'Okay, okay, I invested the money in a development that didn't happen, I didn't see the warning signs, and I made a mistake. I was going to put it back soon. I have other deals going on and I was going to put it all back soon, I promise!'

'I'm your wife!' Jodie spat, 'You're supposed to talk to me, share things with me, especially something as big as this. This isn't just your money,' she screamed, 'this is our money!' She looked at him with disgust in her eyes.

'But I didn't want to bloody worry you for nothing!' Steve retorted, 'I would have put it back, you've got to believe me, Jodie, please!' Steve was all but begging by now.

'Had I not gone to the bank, I would never have bloody known, you bastard!'

He reached for her, 'Jodie…'

'Enough, Steve, I've heard enough, and I can't be near you right now.'

'Jodie, please,' Steve pleaded, but it was no use, Jodie picked up her handbag, walked out of the front door and slammed it behind her. The next few months passed in a blur for Steve, and it took a lot of begging from him, lots of ignored phone calls, lots of talking and lots of tears from them both for Jodie to come back and pick up the pieces. He made it up to her in many ways: took her on exotic holidays, bought her beautiful jewellery, flowers, whatever it took and, eventually, she forgave him. In fact, Steve thought that it had made them stronger in a weird way. They seemed closer, they're lovemaking was even better than before, if that was possible. They discussed everything, laughed like they had always done and had fun days out as a couple and with friends. They shared intimate meals in fancy restaurants and discussed anything and everything. Things were good, very good, so why did Steve still feel sick to the pit of his stomach that something wasn't right.

Christmas Day 1985

Stella didn't see the point of getting up. She had nothing to get up for. No family, no children, not even a pet for company, nothing. Well, that wasn't entirely true. She had Aunt Gabby, but she had reluctantly gone away for Christmas with her boyfriend, Luigi. They'd been together for just over six months, (he was eight years younger than Gabby and Stella joked that she'd found herself a toy boy) and he had taken her to meet his family in Italy. 'I feel terrible leaving you alone at Christmas, Stella, it's not right!' Gabby had protested a week ago.

'I'll be fine, honestly, I'm good,' Stella had replied, hiding how unhappy and pissed off she truly was. She hated feeling this sorry for herself, saw it as a weakness. 'Are you sure, sweetheart?'

'More than sure, you go and have a wonderful time, you deserve it, you work so bloody hard and I want you to relax and enjoy Italy,' Stella replied. Four months earlier, Jason had broken Stella's heart. He'd arranged a picnic in a local park on a beautiful summer's day, champagne, strawberries, the lot and after a couple of glasses, maybe it was to summon up his courage, maybe not, he told her he didn't see a future together and that it was for the best that they end their relationship. She had not seen it coming, no clues, nothing. To say she had been devastated was an understatement. No one else was involved, he had told her, but he was going from strength to strength in his job, and he didn't want to be in a relationship anymore. It was that simple, that brutal.

'Jason, please don't do this,' Stella had pleaded, but it was no good, Jason had made up his mind and even had the nerve to say they could still be friends.

'Stella, I do care about you very much, and I don't want us to part on a bad note. We can still be friends, can't we?' No, they could not be friends, how could he even contemplate this? Jason tried to phone Stella on numerous occasions after delivering his blow, but she wasn't interested. She may have been heartbroken, but she was also very proud. Beth was caught in the middle and felt terrible for Stella but also supported her brother in his decision. Stella felt that it caused a rift in their friendship, and they started to grow apart in some ways, so Stella decided to move out of the flat they shared despite Beth asking her not to.

'Look, Stella, he's my brother, and you are my best friend., What do you want me to say, to do?' Beth had said.

'This isn't about you, Beth, this is about me. I just think it's for the best, okay?' All she took with her were good memories, a royal blue velvet retro sofa she had invested in with her Aunt Gabby's kind donation when she'd moved, four suitcases which contained her worldly belongings and her old banger of a car which she still couldn't bear to part with. Gabby had insisted she move back in with her and had Luigi not been living with Gabby at this point, she may have taken her up on the offer, so she politely declined and rented a one bedroom flat above a fish and chip shop near the office where she worked in Kensington. It took almost all her wages after bills and food, but she liked the area, as it had a really nice cosmopolitan feel and she had made it as homely as she could. She dragged herself out of bed and flicked on the television only to be greeted with smiling children singing Christmas carols. She imagined Jason, Beth and their parents waking up on this Christmas morning, opening their presents, enjoying delicious food and enjoying a family Christmas. Beth had phoned her and wished her a Merry Christmas and told her that Jason wished her the same. Had he met someone? Stella couldn't ask, just the thought of him with someone else had made her feel sick so she'd simply wished Beth a Merry Christmas, too. She was feeling very sorry for herself, afraid and for once in her entire life, and apart from the pain of losing her mother, angry that she was in this place which felt like hell. She walked over to the mantelpiece and picked up a framed photograph of her and her mother. She kissed the photo and whispered, 'I love you, Mum, and I miss you so much.' She wandered into the kitchen and looked in the fridge. Two mince pies, double cream, a cottage pie and a bottle of white wine. Well, at least she had Christmas lunch sorted. No, there was only one thing for it. If she was this pissed off and unhappy, there was only one person who could change her life, Stella herself.

Present day

That evening, she couldn't stop thinking about Steve and Jodie, such a beautiful couple with the world at their feet. At least it seemed that way. Looking at the photograph of Jodie, Stella just knew she'd seen her somewhere before but couldn't remember where and this annoyed her. Maybe she was overtired and needed to relax. 'Bloody grass, I just can't understand why it isn't as green this year,' Roger interrupted her thoughts and she glanced over at him looking out of the window.

'Pardon, what do you mean?' He walked back to the kitchen table and sat down opposite Stella. 'Well, I've done everything I can think of, from planting different seeds to mowing it as I always have done and it doesn't look right, doesn't feel right, it's really aggravating!' As Roger was droning on and on about the grass, it came to her, where she'd seen Jodie before, it was at the garden centre. She was a business partner there and she'd seen her when she and Roger had gone there to buy plants for the garden. She was never really one to involve herself in the customer service side of things, but she had seen Jodie on a handful of occasions chatting to customers and, once or twice, at the till. With her model looks, admirable figure and lifestyle, Stella thought that she was the most unlikely person to be involved in that type of business, but it doesn't really work like that, does it? I mean Stella hardly looked like a private investigator. 5'6, slim, her mousey brown hair cut into an elegant bob. She had been told quite a few times in her life that she was an attractive woman and she took very good care of herself, always had done. She'd never smoked, only drank socially and the odd glass of wine at home with Roger, but she was tough where it mattered, inside and that quality alone made her even better at her job. At least Stella thought so. 'Well, dear, I am sure you'll have it looking beautiful again in no time,' Stella replied, not really interested in grass, seeds or whatever was making him grumpy this evening. 'I have a very busy day tomorrow, Roger, and won't be home until late.'

'Okay, darling, anything interesting?' he replied.

'No, just work, love, just work,' Stella replied.

'I've got a busy day too,' Roger said. 'I have a big job to price up for the couple who bought the Maddison's house, remember, I told you about them? They want a lot done.'

'Yes, they've retired here, haven't they, from Edinburgh? Stella said.

'Yes, that's right,' Roger replied. 'Anyway, I'm meeting Eric for a bite to eat in town.' Eric was Roger's best friend. He'd known him for many years and Eric helped Roger sometimes with big landscaping jobs. He was divorced and Roger's company, not to mention the extra money meant a lot to Eric. 'That will be nice, love, give him my regards, won't you?'

'Of course, I will,' Roger replied. Stella loved every minute of her job. In fact, she really didn't look at it as work as she enjoyed it so much and the money it paid was an added bonus. She was one of the best as she got results and got them fast. That is why her reputation was so damn good.

'I'm off to bed,' Stella said.

'See you up there in a bit,' Roger replied, still annoyed about his beloved grass.

London, 1986

Gabby sat at her desk in her plush office overlooking the Thames when her phone rang. 'Hello?' she said. 'Hello, Bella.' It was Luigi, her boyfriend. He always called her Bella and Gabby found it quite endearing. 'Hey, gorgeous, how are you?'

'I'm good, just wondering what time you'll be home,' he said.

'Ugh, I've got so much on, I'm running behind on a presentation and must stay until it's done,' Gabby said with a frustrated tone in her voice. There was a pause and Luigi said, 'But, baby, I don't get to see you these days, you're always late home and I miss you.'

Here he goes again, she thought, he was always moaning that he didn't get to see her these days. Did he not realise just how stressful and demanding her job was? 'I know, sweetie, but we'll do something nice this weekend, I promise,' she said when she really felt like telling him to not be so immature and needy. It was alright for him. He was an English teacher and was always home at the same time every evening, apart from when he had to stay behind to grade papers from time to time. He had weekends off, he didn't know just how demanding and stressful her job was and if he did, he didn't really show it. 'Okay, Bella, I'll wait up for you and we can have a chat and a glass of wine when you get in.'

'Sounds lovely, see you later,' Gabby said, not really meaning it. She was bloody exhausted and had a pile of papers on her desk to go through, not to mention the presentation which was due imminently. She was pissed off now that she hadn't told him how she really felt but she was just too damn nice, too understanding, too afraid of upsetting him and hurting his feelings. He was eight years younger than her and a great person, funny, kind, intelligent and a great partner but, there was something missing in the relationship. They'd met at Waterloo Station when he'd accidentally bumped into her, knocking the herbal tea she was carrying from her hand.

'I'm so sorry, are you okay?' Luigi went bright red.

'Yes, I'm fine,' she replied. He'd offered to buy her another tea and the rest is history. The Christmas they'd spent at his family home in Italy could not have gone better. His family were wonderful and such lovely people. His mother, also a teacher, had taken Gabby by the hand on Christmas Eve and said, 'My son thinks the world of you. He really does. I've never seen him this happy, Gabby.'

'Oh, he's wonderful,' Gabby had replied. She didn't really feel comfortable discussing their relationship with his mother. No, she had felt this way for some time now and confided in Stella. 'It's so good on so many levels, but I just don't see a future and I can't hurt him, I just don't see us together forever,' she'd told Stella over dinner one evening. 'Nothing is forever, Aunt Gabby,' Stella had replied in her funny, yet to the point way. 'I know, but, well, he loves me so much, tells me all the time and I don't have in me to burst his happy little bubble and break his heart.'

'Well, only you can decide the right thing to say and do, Aunt Gabby,' Stella had told her. Yes, her niece was right. In fact, Stella was right about so many things. Gabby was so incredibly proud of Stella. She loved her with all her heart. Losing Marnie had been devastating for them both and Stella had turned into a wonderful young lady. Her mother would have been so proud. She missed her sister every, single day. It was right what Stella had said. Gabby was the only one that could do something about the Luigi situation, but she hadn't and here they were. 'I'm such a soft cow,' she muttered to herself as she reached over and grabbed a handful of papers.

Present Day

Jodie needed to phone Steve, but she had a million things to do first, one of them being check in on her business partner at the garden centre. She'd invested in the business the previous year and was happy that she had. When she'd taken it on, her family and friends, not to mention her husband, couldn't quite understand it. Business was booming, and as a silent partner, she didn't need to get her hands dirty, just be in the background, have weekly meetings to discuss how things were going and go through the books from time to time, which she enjoyed. She'd only been at front of house on a few occasions, talking to the customers and once or twice, on the till. The business was going from strength to strength and Jodie and her partner, Liz, could not have been happier. It was a miracle that she had managed to invest in the first place as when she went to the bank on that cold wintry day, the shock of finding out that £200,000 pounds were missing from her and Steve's joint account had made her run from the bank where she promptly vomited on the pavement outside. She was shaking so much that she had trouble driving home to confront Steve. It had to be a mistake, it had to be. Her husband would never, ever do anything like this without talking to her about it beforehand. They discussed everything, didn't they? She still remembered the first time she saw him. He was staring at her as she looked at the wine selection at their local wine bar. Although not short of attention from men, she knew that she had Steve there and then. She could tell. When you're that attractive, you just know, it's an instinct. As beautiful as Jodie was, she was by no means conceited. She got her looks from her French mother, she believed. Steve was extremely handsome, tall and strong with a great body and he certainly knew how to conduct himself, not only in business but socially too. Some would say that the night they met was fate. She had been due to meet her friend, Abigail for dinner but she had cancelled at the last minute, so Jodie decided to head to the wine bar instead. That night, they talked over a bottle of her choice of wine, a Chilean red, ate Spanish olives and cheese and laughed as though they had known each other for years. He really was the whole package and wealthy with it too, not that this was important to Jodie, she had her own money. She'd sold a beauty business the year before and had made wise investments with the money. Soon, they were inseparable. They had more in common than they first realised and fell in love very quickly. Although she had had previous relationships, she'd never met anyone like Steve. He treated her like a goddess and was the best lover she had ever had. Their first holiday together in Greece, was spent riding along on their hired moped, laughing hysterically, taking in the sights, eating local produce, drinking cheap, local wine and at night making slow, passionate love, exploring each other's bodies until they fell asleep.

'Jodie, words can't express what I feel for you, what you mean to me, how you have changed me.' Steve had taken her hand on the last day of that blissful holiday as they stood on the edge of the mountain top, the sun disappearing behind the horizon. Then Steve was down on his knee, tears in his eyes, 'Will you marry me, Jodie'

'Yes! Oh my God, yes!' Jodie replied. It was one of the happiest days of her life, but that was then, and this was now. When she found out what Steve had done with "their" money she was beyond furious. She screamed, he begged for forgiveness, she screamed some more and couldn't bear to look at him. When he told her he'd made a dodgy investment and lost all that money, she was so shocked she couldn't speak. She felt so betrayed. Did their marriage mean so little to him? She stormed out that very night and went to stay with her business partner, Liz where she remained for almost two months. She didn't return his calls for over a week, threw the bouquets of flowers he sent her in the bin and got stuck into work at the garden centre every day, getting more involved in the everyday running of it until she finally agreed to meet with Steve to try and salvage their marriage. It had not been easy though. She found it very hard to forgive him and his betrayal ran deep, but they got there in the end.

'Hey! Hi, honey,' Steve replied on his car phone.

'Babe, listen, something's come up, and I can't make the gala dinner tomorrow night.'

'Oh, come on, Jodie, you know how important this is for me!' Steve replied in an angry tone. He had clients flying in from Ireland and wanted to make a good impression. He had always felt invincible with Jodie by his side on important occasions. 'Come on, don't be like that, I have so many things to do and catch up on, honey, please understand,' Jodie replied in a sweet tone. 'Not only that, I've been to so many of them before, not having me there isn't the end of the world.' Steve knew she was right, it would be boring anyway, he'd be talking business most of the evening, but as he was feeling low, he just felt that she could have made the effort.

'Okay, I understand, never mind, don't worry,' he mumbled somewhat unconvincing.

'Are you sure you're okay about it, babe? I know I should have told you sooner, but I forgot. I haven't seen Rachel for so long and she's called me and will be in town tomorrow for a fleeting visit, you know how much she means to me and I really want to see her, we've got so much catching up to do.'

'Yeah, babe, don't worry. It's fine. You would probably find it boring anyway.'

'Love you, gorgeous, and I'll see you at home in a bit, okay,' Jodie said.

'Yeah, love you too, see you soon.'

'Bye, darling!' and Jodie hung up. The heavy rain made it hard for Steve to see through the windscreen and the sudden boom of thunder made him jump. A storm is coming he thought to himself and the pounding in his chest told him it wasn't just the weather.

Cornwall, April 1987

It was Aunt Gabby's idea that they both have a long weekend away at the cottage to recharge their batteries and enjoy the outdoors. Not long after Gabby had returned from Italy with Luigi, she had confided in Stella that their relationship wasn't really going anywhere and had put it down to the age gap. 'I mean he's great, good fun, his family were really lovely, but I'm just not really feeling it,' she'd told Stella over a bottle of white wine at her flat.

'Do you love him?' Stella had asked.

'I really like him a lot and we have fun together, but I think he's more into me, than me him. Oh, I feel like a right bitch!' Gabby had said, taking a gulp of wine.

'Aunt Gabby, if you're not happy, then you're not happy, that's what you're always telling me.'

'How come you got to be so smart?' Gabby replied, placing her hand over Stella's. But, Gabby being Gabby, she had tried to make the relationship work, but it wasn't to be, and she had finally found the courage to ask Luigi to move out of her flat. Two months earlier, a tearful Luigi had moved out, begging her to change her mind, but she had remained strong, told him it was for the best and that he would realise it in the end, and she hugged him goodbye. So here they were, sitting on the large terrace with beautiful views of the sea enjoying a weekend away together.

'I've got a landscape gardener popping round to take a look and to brighten up the place a bit for me,' Gabby told Stella over dinner. 'He's local and has a fantastic reputation. You should see some of the work he's done, so talented!'

'It looks good to me already,' Stella had replied, not really understanding what all the hype for one to have an immaculate garden was all about. Stella and plants did not get along. She, somehow, always managed to kill them. She remembered a plant she and Beth were given as a housewarming gift, when they'd first moved in. It was a lovely plant, its leaves green and vibrant, yet within a month, despite both her and Beth taking, what they thought was good care of it, it had shrivelled to nothing, its leaves hanging down like a queen who had been revoked of her crown. The next day, while Gabby and gone into town to run some errands, Roger, the landscape gardener had arrived.

'Do you fancy a tea or coffee?' Stella had asked him.

'Coffee would be great, thank you, one sugar, please.'

'Aunt Gabby will be back soon, she just had to pop out.'

'No worries' Roger replied. 'It's a beautiful house, the views are great.'

'Yeah, it is, Aunt Gabby loves it here and I've been coming here since I was little.' There was an awkward silence before they heard the key in the door and Gabby walked in. 'Roger, I'm so sorry, I really thought I'd be back sooner!' Gabby said in an apologetic tone. 'Don't worry, honestly. It's fine.' Was Stella just imagining it, or did she notice that Roger was staring at her? 'Anyway, let me show you what I have in mind.' Gabby said, leading Roger out onto the terrace. 'I mean, you're the expert, but I've drawn a few pictures as to what I think would look good, different,' Gabby said to Roger.

'Of course,' Roger said, looking at Gabby's drawings. 'Well, nice to meet you, Stella,' Roger said as he followed her Aunt outside. 'Yes, you too,' she replied. There was something awkward about him, Stella thought but he seemed nice. Half an hour later, Gabby entered the house, a smile on her face. 'Well, I think you've made an impression today, young lady.'

'What?' replied Stella.

'Roger, he was asking questions about you. I mean he's quite shy, but I think he was hinting at asking you out.'

'Aunt Gabby, please, you and your imagination.' Gabby started chuckling to herself as she walked to the kitchen. The next day, Roger returned to the house with drawings and a quote for Gabby. 'Wow, this is stunning, Roger!' Gabby had declared when she saw them. 'It's everything I had in mind and more.' Roger glanced over in Stella's direction and gave her a smile. *Lovely smile*, Stella had thought.

'I know you're a very busy young man but as soon as you can start, that would be great, I'm so impressed, I really am.'

'I'm fully booked for a month or so, but after that, I'm all yours.'

'Great, I'm really excited about it all. It's going to look amazing?' Gabby replied.

'If you're not busy tonight, I was wondering if you'd like to have dinner with me,' Roger said to Stella when Gabby had gone off to get her cheque book for the deposit.

'Sure, I'm not busy; that would be nice, thank you.' Stella replied, taken aback somewhat.

'Great, I'll pick you up at seven, if that's okay?'

'Sure, I'll be ready, see you then,' Stella replied, feeling, for some reason, like a teenager. The restaurant was lovely, small and quaint but very nice all the same. Although Stella felt they were very different, they had hit it off. He was 25, two years older than Stella, had his own business, lived in town in his own flat and loved what he did. He was fascinated by Stella's life in London, she too was now working for herself as a private investigator and he found this fascinating. She had decided to leave her job the previous year. She had worked her way up throughout the years with them and, with the support from the law firm, acquired the necessary qualifications to become a private investigator. In fact, it was one of her bosses, Mr Giles who had mentioned it to her in the first place. 'Stella, you're an intelligent woman, you've got an eye for things and a nose to know when something isn't right! We've all noticed it since you've worked for us and this combination is what makes a great private investigator. You're very discreet but tough.' She'd been incredibly flattered and quite humbled that they felt this way and didn't want to let them down. More importantly, she didn't want to let herself down and she'd studied hard every evening, late into the night, on weekends, politely declining nights out with her colleagues and the sacrifice had paid off. She, along with a lot of moral support from Mr Giles and his partners at the law firm, had passed all the exams with flying colours. They were sorry to see her go but understood her reasons. Money was very tight at first as she only had her savings and still had to pay rent and bills, so she worked from her flat. She had an old computer and a secondhand filing cabinet she'd found in a local charity shop, but word soon got around and before long, she had built up a client base and rented a small office space in an insurance building. Seeing her name, in gold lettering on the glass pane for the first time had made her feel very proud. **Stella Matthews, PRIVATE INVESTIGATOR.** There was something very endearing about Roger. They were total opposites in many ways, but she found him very sweet and his shyness against her outgoingness made her smile. There was most definitely a spark. He was tall and had short, brown hair and blue eyes. Yes, he was very good looking. The meal was delicious and when he dropped her off at Gabby's later that night, they had arranged to meet the following day.

'Thank you, Roger, I've had a lovely evening and lunch is on me tomorrow, okay?'

'If you insist,' he had smiled. His smile was amazing, sincere. The following day, they'd walked along the beach talking about anything and everything and enjoyed fish and chips at a restaurant near the beach. When they had kissed outside the house before she left to go back to London with Gabby on Sunday evening, she felt her heart flutter for the first time since Jason. It wasn't long before they were seeing each other every weekend and sometimes, he'd drive up to London to be with her, when work permitted, during the week. They'd go to the theatre, walk along the embankment, eat at lovely restaurants and visit historical landmarks together. She liked being with Roger and spending time with him. He made her feel safe. He made her feel wanted. He also made her feel good about herself and was a very good listener. The first time they'd made love, he had been very caring and sensual, put her needs first. He was a good lover and she couldn't help herself comparing him to how it had been with Jason. Roger was a very sensitive and caring lover, whereas, with Jason, it had been passionate and had left her wanting more. Roger and Jason were just different people. That was all.

Present Day

Roger prepared his breakfast, two poached eggs on toast and a strong cup of coffee and thought about Stella. She was always up before him these days, rushing around and not really taking care of herself. He can't remember the last time they'd enjoyed a long, leisurely breakfast together. He was so proud of her though and she was the best at what she did, that's why he didn't see much of her these days. She always had cases to solve and people to see. When they'd first met, he was in awe of her, of her intelligence, her drive, her lust for life. Now, he just wished she would slow down from time to time. Was it just his imagination, or had she been particularly snappy at him lately?

'No, I'm being paranoid,' he said out loud. Since he'd met Stella, all those years ago, he had most definitely come out of his shell, was more confident and outgoing which, in turn, had made him feel more alive and ready to take on what life had to throw his way. He had been very shy as a young boy unlike his brother Mark. They'd lived in so many wonderful countries though due to their father serving in the army. His favourite had been Singapore. Beautiful climate, history, food, people, yes, he had loved Singapore. They'd moved there when Roger was in his teens but just when he'd felt settled, it was time to move on, typical. Roger was very close to his mother, Sue, and although he loved his father, Brian, he wouldn't say they were close. His dad was very strict and never showed any emotion. 'Sue, Roger needs to go out more and do the things that boys do, he's always in here reading books, or with you in the garden!' he heard him bellow one summer's morning in their large kitchen at the house in Singapore. 'Oh, Brian, leave him alone, he's a good kid, he loves reading and helping me outside, what's wrong with that?' His father grunted. 'At least he's not out there causing trouble like some boys his age,' his mum had argued in a protective tone. 'And anyway, he's a big help to me in the garden and very talented, may I add.' His mother smiled at Roger and he smiled back. Roger thought that was where his passion for the outside had started. Their garden in Singapore was beautiful and Roger had spent many days in the sunshine planting different flowers, plants and trees. When they'd moved in, Roger was mesmerised by a majestic flowering tree called the Frangipani, which was commonly seen in Buddhist or Hindu temples and associated with death in the Malay custom. When Roger had moved back to Cornwall, he knew his future had to be in horticulture, and after graduating from university, he'd soon started his own landscape business which had proved to be very successful and profitable. He had attended university, and within his first semester, met his girlfriend, Grace. Although Roger's parents had been very generous and helped him out with university fees, money was still quite tight, so he found himself sharing a house to save money. Grace fitted her name, petite, blonde, pretty and very graceful. For a drama student, Grace was quite introvert, like Roger but she was very talented. They'd met when Roger had moved into where Grace was living with her flatmates, Teddy and Julie. Roger had fancied Grace straight away. Within two months, they were sharing a bedroom and life was one big adventure of classes, studying, partying, and so on. Teddy and Julie were art students and nice people. Teddy was single and a party animal and Julie was a lesbian who, much to the annoyance of Grace and Roger, brought home a different girl every weekend. "You only live once" was her motto. In fact, she had this quote tattooed on her shoulder. She was good fun though and a good friend and housemate. Roger studied hard and enjoyed all his classes and university life in general. He got very good grades, and when he visited his parents, he could tell they were proud of him, even his father.

'Roger, I think we should think about getting a place of our own at some point in the near future,' Grace said one evening when they were on their own in the house eating dinner. 'Really, of our own, what's wrong with it here?' Roger had replied. 'Nothing, I mean I love Teddy and Julie to bits, but it feels like we're on top of each other at times, apart from when we're in our room,' Grace had replied with a cheeky smile. She was a right little minx when she wanted to be. 'We can't really afford to move out, Grace, it's expensive as it is and we get to have our own time together, don't we?'

'Yeah, I know, but it would just be nice to have our own place to entertain, be alone, you know…' Grace trailed off.

'Babe, really, it's okay here, for now; we're all under stress what with exams coming up. It's not the time, not yet.'

'Okay, point taken,' Grace had said, not really meaning it. That night, Roger was tired. He'd been studying really hard, but they'd still made love. Grace's sexual appetite was something else! He wasn't complaining but to say she was insatiable was an understatement. As she lay in his arms, Grace had whispered, 'I didn't mean to freak you out today, babe, you know, about the moving out thing, it's just that I want us to be together and have our own little place.'

   'I know, Grace, me too, it's just that now is not the right time.' She looked deep into his eyes, kissed him gently and whispered, 'I do love you, Roger.' Three months later, Roger had just found out his exam results and rushed back to the flat to tell Grace his good news. He'd passed with flying colours and not only that, had been to the estate agents and put a deposit down on a one bedroom flat in town for them. He'd thought long and hard about what Grace had said, about getting a place of their own and having borrowed some money from his parents, had secretly been looking at places for them. Flowers and champagne in hand, he couldn't wait to get back to tell her the good news. He turned the key in the lock and opened the door. The sight of a naked Grace on top of his naked flatmate, Teddy, on the sofa made him drop the champagne in his hand. It fell to the floor and shattered. 'Oh, fuck, Roger!' Grace cried, leaping up and frantically grabbing her clothes. Roger stood there, rooted to the spot, numb. 'Roger, mate, it's not what it looks like,' said a bumbling Teddy behind her. Yet Roger continued to stand there, like a complete idiot, just staring at the pair of them running this way and that like a pair of headless chickens. 'Babe, please. Say something!' Grace was crying now, frantically putting on her clothes as Teddy disappeared to his room. By now, Grace was crying her eyes out, pulling at Roger's arm to sit down. But it was like Roger was watching her from another place, from outside himself, in slow motion. He actually felt quite calm despite the scene that had just unfolded before him moments ago. By now, Grace was shaking him, 'Babe, talk to me, talk to me, please! She was pleading. 'It was a mistake. I don't know what to say, please, Roger, I love you.' Roger looked at her, and she looked pathetic, eyes swollen, tears streaming down her face, lips quivering, pathetic. What on earth had he seen in her? She was nothing but a slut. 'Grace, you and Teddy are welcome to each other. Go to hell.' With that, he abruptly removed her hand from his arm and walked out of the flat. Who in the hell did he think she was, treating him like that? He was not going to be treated like that, by anyone, ever again. 'I will be here tomorrow getting my things together, and I don't want you here, do you understand?' He liaised with Julie over the following days, arranging to go to the flat when Grace was out. Julie didn't want to be in the middle, and he understood that, but she was on his side as to the way Teddy and Grace had behaved. Grace kept trying to call him and wait for him after his classes, but he had ignored all her calls and didn't want to see her ever again. He had nothing to say to her. He moved back to Cornwall shortly after having achieved his degree and never heard from Grace again. He'd never really loved her though, not really. He'd been swept along by a boy's young dream of what he thought love was at the time. No, Roger had never loved anyone properly until he'd met Stella.

Cornwall, July 1988

Stella hated the smell that hit your nostrils when you entered the hospital. As clean as it was, that smell was always there, pungent, clinical and for the past six months, all too familiar. Her mind wandered back to that bitterly cold morning in January. 'Stella, I have something important to tell you.' Gabby was shaking as she asked Stella to sit down and Stella, seeing the look on her aunt's face, started to feel very uneasy. 'Aunt Gabby, you're scaring me.'

'It's okay, sweetheart. It's okay.' She took Stella's hand into her own and uttered the words, 'I've got cancer.' Stella remembered staring at her aunt in disbelief as she let the words wash over her.

'What?'

'It's cancer, darling, lung cancer.' Stella noticed Gabby was trying not to cry, trying to be brave.

'Why?' was all Stella could say, 'I mean you don't smoke, you're healthy, you eat well, don't drink much.'

'I know, I know, I've asked the same question a hundred times but there is no explanation, I've just been unlucky.'

'How long have you known?'

'About a month or so,' Gabby replied.

'You've kept this to yourself for a month?'

'I didn't want to worry you, sweetheart, I know you've got a lot on your plate what with planning the wedding, your job, Roger…' she trailed off. Stella felt as though she'd been punched in the stomach with a sledgehammer and could not hold back her tears. They cried together and held onto each other as though they would never let go. Now, here they were, almost seven months on and it was time for Stella to put on her brave face once again as she got out of the lift and headed to where her aunt lay riddled with cancer.

'Hey, you, how are you feeling?'

'Hello, sweetheart.' Gabby's gaunt, ghostly face stared up from the hospital bed as she attempted a weak smile. 'Here, let me fluff your pillow for you.' She lifted her aunt from the bed, and it was like lifting a skeleton. She was so frail, completely bald and a mere shadow of her former self. Stella made her comfortable and they chatted about this and that. She had a private hospital room which was filled with beautiful vases of flowers, cards and with a nice view of the hospital gardens. Chemotherapy, radiotherapy and other endless tests had left Gabby so very weak. Stella had been by her aunt's side since the diagnosis, held her long, blonde hair back as she had vomited violently from all the treatment, held her close when she had sobbed uncontrollably and watched her sleep, petrified that she wouldn't wake up. The week before, she had been told by her oncologist that there was nothing more they could do. It was terminal. Stella had been devastated.

'How long?' she had asked.

'Three months, maybe four, it's hard to tell for sure,' her oncologist, Dr Rivers had replied. 'We will do everything to ensure she is as comfortable as possible and pain-free.' That evening, she had sat Roger down and told him that she wanted to bring their wedding forward. Aunt Gabby had to be there and if they went with the original date, she wouldn't be, according to what her oncologist had said. 'Of course, darling,' Roger replied, holding her close. 'Whatever needs to be done, whatever it takes, we'll do.' Stella broke free from his embrace and instantly felt guilty when she saw the look on his face.

'Sorry, Roger, I just can't take it in.'

'I know, honey, I know, it's just awful, I can't believe it either.' Roger and Gabby were close, and she knew he was hurting too. 'I'm here for you and we're in everything together, you do know that don't you?' Stella took his hand and said, 'Yes, I know that; of course, I do, thank you.' She gave Roger a weak smile. 'I just need a bit of fresh air,' she said. She walked from the living room and on to the terrace outside. The terrace that had brought Roger and Stella together, thanks to her beautiful aunt. The beautifully landscaped terrace that Roger kept pristine with colourful flowers and plants, the terrace where she and Gabby had spent many a summer's evening talking through their fears, sharing their secrets and laughed until they thought they could laugh no more. She felt afraid, alone and so angry that she began screaming at the top of her lungs then fell on her knees to the ground and sobbed.

Present Day

That night, Stella had a vivid dream. She was about nine or 10 and was with her mother walking along the beach. It was raining and the sky was black. She looked up at her mum and noticed that she was crying. 'Mummy, what's wrong, why are you crying?'

'Darling, I have to go soon, it's time for me to go soon,' her mother replied in the dream.

'Can I come with you, Mummy?'

'No, sweetheart, it's not your time yet.'

'Time for what, Mummy?' At that moment, a big wave came towards them, and they were swept away. Stella found it hard to breathe and started screaming for her mum who had disappeared beneath the waves. She then saw Roger, looking at her from the shore. 'Help me, please help me,' Stella called out, but Roger turned his back and started to walk away from the shore waving at her as he went. As she descended into the murky, lashing waves, Gabby took her in her arms and then

41

next thing she knew, she was back on the shore with Roger by her side. He had a sad expression on his face, and she hugged him tightly. 'Where's my mummy, where's Aunt Gabby?' Stella asked Roger.

'Oh, my love, my Stella, they're gone,' he had a sinister look on his face now and Stella felt very scared. 'You'll never see them again, nothing lasts forever.' Roger started laughing with an evil look on his face. 'They're gone, Stella, nothing lasts forever, you should know this by now.' He let her go and she fell back into the icy cold sea. Stella woke up with a start and was coughing. She reached over for the glass of water on her bedside table and took a gulp. 'Shit, shit,' she muttered in the darkness. 'What a horrible dream.'

August 1988

Beth had arrived in Cornwall a couple of weeks before the wedding to help Stella with everything. She was staying with Stella and was to be her only bridesmaid. She was engaged to Stuart, a plasterer from London. She hadn't changed much and was now a manager at a big department store on Oxford Street. She was still into her fashion and had arrived the night before wearing a bizarre ensemble of blue trousers, paisley shirt and velvet boots. 'It's so good to see you, Stella,' she had said, hugging her friend close. 'It's been too long, hasn't it?'

'Yes, it has, it has,' Stella replied.

'How's Gabby?' Beth asked, placing her hand on Stella's arm.

'Oh, Beth, she's not good at all, it breaks my heart seeing her like this. It's just awful.' Stella could feel herself getting upset and changed the subject. 'How are Jason and his wife and baby daughter?' Stella asked, a little too eagerly.

'They're all good, yes.' Beth had replied a little awkwardly. 'He sends his love and best wishes to you both.' Yes, Jason had indeed climbed the career ladder. He was now in CID and from what Beth said, enjoying every minute. For one, brief moment, Stella felt betrayed that not long after breaking off their relationship, he had started seeing a fellow colleague, and within two years, he was married. 'Roger's a great guy, Stella,' Beth said, interrupting her train of thought.

'Yeah, he is. We're very different, but we just get on, you know?' Not long after they had become engaged, they had talked about Stella wanting to keep her maiden name and Roger had completely understood this. There was no way she could lose Matthews altogether. 'I don't want to lose that bond, Roger. It's the only thing that still ties me to my mum.'

'I know, darling,' Roger had replied. 'Do whatever makes you happy, and hey, a double barrel name is cool, don't you think, very sophisticated! Mrs Stella Sinclair-Matthews,' he had said with pride. Roger was so very different to Jason but that was a long time ago and this was now. 'I really miss you in London, but I have to say, you seem very settled here and it's absolutely beautiful, isn't it?' Beth said to her.

'Oh, it is. The fresh air alone makes all the difference and I do love it here. Apart from the shops and you, of course, I can honestly say I really don't miss London that much.' Beth looked at her friend and thought back to all their times together in London when they were younger and smiled. 'Your mum would be so proud of you, Stella, you've achieved so much and gone through a lot, she'd be incredibly proud of you.' What her friend said to her brought a tear to Stella's eyes and she smiled fondly at her oldest friend. 'Do you really think so?'

'Absolutely, without a shadow of a doubt, she was a wonderful woman and loved you so very much, I could see that when we were kids, the way she looked at you, the way she laughed when you played together.'

'Beth, I miss her so much it hurts,' Stella replied as a single tear rolled down her cheek.

'I know you do, sweetie, I know you do,' Beth replied.

Present day

When Stella woke up the following morning, she felt tired and still quite shaken about the dream, or was it a nightmare she'd had? She hoped she wasn't coming down with a cold or something. She felt exhausted and her chest felt tight. She hoped it wasn't a panic attack coming on. She'd suffered with those years back. Still, she was up very early, before Roger, who was sleeping soundly. She looked at him, at his expanding waistline and really wished she could show her appreciation more, not be as snappy or bossy and try and retrieve some of the magic that had long gone from their marriage. Roger did look after himself. He ate a healthy diet and kept fit with all his gardening work, but he had gained a little weight over the past couple of years. She felt as though she didn't appreciate him how she should of late or maybe that was just the tiredness talking. She knew he adored her, he told her every day, and this thought alone made her smile. Roger had always been very supportive of her job which often left her away from the house for hours on end. She shouldn't have been so curt with him the previous evening and she felt bad about it. Within two hours, Stella was parked at a safe distance from Jodie's car while Jodie was shopping at a nearby parade of expensive shops and plush boutiques. It was normal stuff, really, nothing out of the norm. It was when she was sitting in her car, feeling a little guilty at the way she had been with him, that she decided to phone Roger to ask him to book their favourite Italian restaurant for the following evening that she'd realised that she didn't have her phone with her. She looked inside her handbag, her briefcase, but it wasn't there. Blast! She remembered now. She put it on the hallstand as she was putting on her coat. Shit! It was the first time she'd left her phone behind and felt weird without it. There was no way she was going back for it now. She would talk to Roger when she got home later, and they could book the restaurant for the following evening. Jodie emerged from one of the expensive boutiques, shopping bags in hand, opened the boot and placed the bags inside. She got in and started the engine, and Stella followed her closely. She drove about a mile or so down the road and parked outside a trendy restaurant. It was a new place, hadn't been open that long. It looked very nice, and Stella thought that maybe she and Roger could give it a try. An attractive woman with long, blonde hair and slim figure greeted her and they hugged affectionately outside the restaurant, both smiling at each other and from what Stella could hear, complimenting each other on how they looked. They went inside and sat by the window. A couple of hours later, they were still chatting away and Stella, momentarily, considered calling it a day as so far, she'd not really seen anything unusual. No, Jodie's movements today were by no means cause for concern. Stella had the classical music station on and was eating a sandwich. She counted her blessings. Being married to Roger was by no means exciting and she did treat him with disdain at times, but she knew he would do anything for her and always went along with what made her happy. She was shaken from her thoughts as Jodie, along with the attractive lady, left the restaurant and hugged each affectionately before she waved Jodie goodbye and went on her way. As Jodie walked back to her car, Stella saw her reach inside her clutch bag to answer her phone. A huge smile appeared on Jodie's face, and she started to laugh with whoever was on the other end. There was an air about her as she chatted happily away. Stella wondered if it was her husband, Steve as she seemed very at ease and carefree. Whoever it was, was making her laugh, this much was for sure. Jodie crossed the road, still on her phone, opened her car door and got inside. She hung up a couple of seconds later and started her engine, as did Stella. 'Right, let's see what happens now,' Stella said to herself out loud.

September 1988

Roger and Stella's wedding day was a quiet affair and only close friends and relatives had been invited. The original date had been set for December 12th, but due to Gabby's deterioration, both Stella and Roger had brought it forward. Gabby's oncologist had also thought it a good idea and Gabby was delighted that she would get to share her beloved niece's day. 'You don't know how happy I am for you, Roger's a wonderful man, he adores you, he loves you and you're just perfect for each other,' Gabby had told Stella the morning of the wedding. By now, Stella had moved to Cornwall on a permanent basis and was working from her aunt's house. In fact, she practically lived at the hospital, not wanting to leave her aunt's side. She had given up the lease on her flat and office space in London not long after Gabby's diagnosis. Also, she had declined several cases as she couldn't concentrate. 'Aunt Gabby, are you sure you feel okay to come to the church?'

'Just you try and stop me. I wouldn't miss it for the world!' Gabby had replied.'

'Stella, your mum would be so incredibly proud of you today, not just today but with everything you have become.'

'I know, Aunt Gabby, I know, I wish she could be here' Stella had replied, not wanting to cry.

'She is here, sweetheart, and she'll be by your side throughout your life, as will I.'

'Aunt Gabby, I want to cancel the honeymoon.'

'I won't be able to enjoy it knowing you're here alone and Roger agrees with me.'

'Now you listen to me, young lady, I will not hear of it, do you understand!' Gabby had replied quite angrily.

'But…!'

'But nothing, you've been by my side night and day and been there with me every step of the way. This is your time now and you and Roger are getting on that plane!' Gabby had replied. Gabby was given stronger painkillers than normal on the day and had chosen a cream dress to wear. It hung off her tiny frame, but she still looked lovely. She was still Aunt Gabby to Stella. Her spirit was still that of a fighter. She was in her wheelchair and Brian, Roger's dad, pushed her to the front of the church to sit alongside him and his wife, Sue and his brother, Mark. His parents had flown in from Spain and were very proud and happy for them both. They were good people. Stella had invited some of the old colleagues from the law firm along with Mr Giles. She'd stayed in touch with them after she had left. The church was set on a hillside overlooking the sea. It was a warm day and the guests looked at Stella as she walked down the aisle with her white, flowing dress. The look on Roger's face was one of love and pride. As she approached him at the altar, she could see he was trying to not let his emotions get the better of him.

'Wow, you look so beautiful,' he had whispered to her as she gazed up at him. Although her heart was breaking inside, she did feel wonderful and happy on her special day. After their vows, they kissed and walked hand in hand back out of the church to be greeted with "CONGRATULATIONS" and confetti. The party lasted into the early hours and as Stella made love to her husband that night, as man and wife, she had felt very lucky and very blessed.

Present Day

Roger finished his breakfast, washed the dishes and looked out of the kitchen window and his, or their rather, immaculate garden. He was worried about Stella. She was not herself lately. She always seemed to be rushing around here and there. He was worried she was taking on too much. He knew she loved her work and, due to her success, she just didn't seem to make time for herself, or for him, for that matter. When they'd first started seeing each other and he would visit her in London, her phone wouldn't stop ringing. 'Wow, you're so popular,' he would tease, and they would laugh together about it. 'Darling, you should just learn to relax a little more,' he had said to her days earlier after she had snapped at him for putting a china teacup and saucer in the dishwasher. 'Everyone knows you don't put china in a dishwasher, Roger!' she had snapped. It was just her way, he knew that; she didn't mean anything by it, but it hurt him all the same. She was so caring in many ways and would do anything for anybody, but her moods did upset him. Before they married, they had discussed the possibility of having children. 'I've never really felt maternal or anything. I mean, losing my mum, I don't know, it scares me.' Stella found it hard to talk about her feelings although he did know that losing her mother at a young age and in such devastating circumstances had, understandably, affected her very deeply. 'Maybe you'll change your mind though, honey. I don't really want to start a family straight away, but who knows what the future holds, eh?' he had replied.

'Yes, maybe, who knows?' But it was not to be. He would have liked to have had the chance to become a father. They really didn't discuss it much after they were married and he didn't want to push her, but Roger couldn't help but wonder if having a child may have softened his wife somewhat, made her less critical of things that really were not that important in life. Maybe he was just too sensitive. Maybe, just maybe, this was the problem. After all, his father had always told him so. Maybe he was annoying. His little habits probably annoyed Stella. He walked out into the garden and felt proud of how beautiful it looked. This was all his doing. Stella had no interest in gardening although she had gone with him on various occasions to the garden centre. He loved it though. It relaxed him and he knew he was incredibly good at it and it had always had a good imagination as to what would look good. He enjoyed being outside in the fresh air plus he got paid very good money to turn other peoples' gardens into something beautiful. 'Do you know, we could probably retire in a couple of years,' he had joked to Stella one evening not so long ago, 'We've got savings, my flat is rented, the flat's rented in London, you know…' Stella had looked at him as though he were mad. 'I don't think so, Roger, really, you are funny.' He had a lot to do today and despite reminiscing about what could have been, he felt excited at what today had to bring. The phone was ringing, and he went back inside and answered it.

October 1988

After their wonderful honeymoon in Thailand, Stella and Roger returned to Cornwall and the news was not good. Aunt Gabby was deteriorating rapidly. Stella wanted her to come home. As her oncologist had said, there was nothing more they could do, and Stella wanted Gabby to be in the home she loved. She would take care of her she had insisted, along with the nurses who would visit daily. It could be done. Money was not a problem and it was what Gabby wanted too. They had rearranged her room at the house to make her comfortable and she and Stella would sit for hours, talking about anything and everything. 'I want to let you know that I've put all my plans in order with my solicitor, Stella. It's all yours, the flat in London and this house, that's what I want. You could maybe rent out the flat in London. It would bring you a good income.'

'Aunt Gabby, please, not now.'

'There's never a good time for this conversation, Stella.' Gabby said, laughing softly. As ill as she was, she still had her humour. 'You've been like a daughter to me and I love you with everything I have. I know you love it here as much as I do, I'm just so glad I got to spend this time here, as ill as I've been, it's been wonderful being here, in this beautiful place, it's always held a very special place in my heart and now it's where you and Roger can create happy memories together.'

'I don't know what to say, Aunt Gabby.'

'Say thank you, Aunt Gabby,' she replied with a grin as she took Stella's hand into her own and they looked out to sea. Exactly three days later, on a beautiful autumnal Sunday, whilst sitting on her beloved terrace which had been lovingly landscaped by Roger only a year or so earlier, Gabby took her last breath as Stella held her hand. She was 42.

Present Day

Steve had been busy all day and was exhausted. He'd been to meeting after meeting which seemed to have gone on for hours and this had put him in a bad mood, and he was feeling incredibly anxious. He didn't know why, he just did. It had taken him longer to get home than normal due to the heavy rain, and he was very angry with himself for having met Stella Sinclair-Matthews at the café in town. Had he thought things through, he wouldn't have allowed himself to have gone through with it, but it was too late now. Stella had everything she needed to be getting on with her "case" or as Steve now thought of it, *Following my beautiful wife, watching her every move, invading her right to do what she wants, when she wants just because I have a stupid hunch that something isn't right.* When he had finally got home, Jodie was in the kitchen drinking a glass of red wine.

'Hi, babe,' she said, planting a kiss on his lips. 'Awful bloody evening, I could barely see on the way home.'

'Me neither. There's one hell of a storm out there,' he had replied. Jodie looked amazing. She was wearing a figure-hugging black dress, red high heels and had her dark hair swept up in a ponytail. 'Steve, you okay?'

'Yes, fine, I just feel tired, that's all.'

She walked towards him and wrapped her arms around his neck. 'Oh, honey, you do look worn out, hard day at work?'

'Yeah, you could say that.' She smelt amazing; she always did whether she was dressed up to the nines or relaxing in sweatpants around the house.

'You are okay with me not being at the gala dinner tomorrow night, aren't you?'

He had forgotten about it to be honest. 'Yes, don't worry, as I said, it'll be boring, most likely.'

'I'll come to the next one, I promise.' She smiled at him and walked upstairs. He walked to the cupboard, took out a wine glass and poured himself a glass of wine. His phone rang and it made him jump. It was his secretary wanting to know who was going to be sitting at his table the following evening. 'No, Jodie's not coming, she can't make it,' he had said, maybe a little sarcastically. 'Yes, that's fine, put me next to Mr Phelps, no problem, okay, yeah, see you in the morning.' Jodie came back downstairs in grey sweatpants, a baggy top and looked just as gorgeous. 'Fancy a takeaway, babe?'

'Sure,' Steve replied. Jodie wasn't really one to cook, it was usually Steve who did all the cooking and tonight, he just couldn't be bothered. After their Chinese takeaway that evening, they lay together on the couch watching a documentary about whales on the tele and Steve couldn't help but feel guilty about having met Stella earlier that morning. It was really playing on his mind. 'Babe,' Jodie said, why don't we plan a little trip away somewhere soon, I don't know, Paris, maybe?'

'Paris?' Steve said.

'Yes, I love it there, and it holds fond memories for us, doesn't it?' she said, snuggling into him. It certainly did hold great memories. They'd spent the weekend there a couple of years back and barely left their hotel room. 'Great, I'll look into it tomorrow.' She looked up at him with a look he'd seen many times before and he knew what was coming next. They made love there and then which left them both breathless. As they lay naked in each other's arms, Steve knew what he had to do, he would phone Stella Sinclair-Matthews the following day and tell her not to go ahead. He was being paranoid, stupid and irrational. If Jodie found out what he had done, she would be furious not to mention deeply hurt that he didn't trust her. She loved him, after all the upset from the year before, all he had put her through, Jodie loved him and that was that.

December 1988

It had been just over two months since Stella had said a final goodbye to her beloved Aunt Gabby. She had been a wreck at the funeral, a blubbering mess. Roger had been amazing. Taken care of all the arrangements, flowers, guests, everything. He had been her rock through this very dark time. He'd held her when she cried, listened to her when she needed to talk to him and gone with her to the solicitor's office when all the paperwork had been dealt with. 'As you know, your aunt's wishes were for you to be her sole heir.'

'Yes,' Stella had replied quietly.

'Everything is going through now, the paperwork, Probate and all.'

'Thank you,' Stella had said. 'There is one thing your aunt wanted you to have.' The solicitor proceeded to hand Stella an envelope with "Stella" written on the front.

'What's this?' Stella asked. He cleared his throat and said, 'It's a letter from your mother.' For a moment, Stella thought she had misheard him. 'I'm sorry.' The solicitor looked slightly uncomfortable and started fidgeting in his big, leather armchair. 'It's a letter your mother left for you, the day she,' he hesitated, 'the day she died.'

'Suicide note?' Stella said, not recognising her own voice.

'Yes,' the solicitor replied. Roger took his wife's hand and squeezed it gently. 'Honey, are you okay?'

'Yes, I'm fine.' But she wasn't fine, she wasn't fine at all. Why had Aunt Gabby not told her about this before, she'd had so many opportunities, so many years to give her what was now in the palm of her hand, why now? She heard a distant thumping sound and realised it was her heart pounding inside her chest.

Present Day

Steve was up very early the next morning and left Jodie sleeping soundly. God, even asleep she was beautiful. Their lovemaking the night before, on the couch, had relaxed Steve and he'd slept very well. He was even more determined to phone Stella and call the whole thing off. It was too early though, only 06:45. No, he couldn't phone her at this hour. He would wait until he reached his office. He showered, went downstairs and made a cup of strong coffee. He had a very busy day ahead consisting of meetings, lunch with a property developer to discuss a new complex they were working on together and then in the evening, the gala dinner which he would be attending alone. This thought irritated him, but he just had to get on with it. Jodie would not be accompanying him. He just had to deal with it. He noticed Jodie's phone on the worktop and saw that there was a message flashing. He couldn't help himself and he didn't know why he did it, but he reached over and picked up the phone and opened the message. *"Hi Jodie, really looking forward to seeing you tomorrow, but I may be a bit late. The restaurant looks amazing! I drove past earlier today. It's really trendy and funky! Anyway, see you soon and can't wait for a good, old catch up, it's been ages! See you soon."* Rachel xxx

Rachel was Jodie's best friend. She'd been chief bridesmaid at their wedding but had moved to Scotland and was in town visiting her parents. Jodie had told him this the previous evening and she was excited at the prospect of seeing her best friend. 'It feels like I haven't seen her in ages, we've so much to catch up on!' Jodie had exclaimed, excitement in her voice. Shit, what had he done? Jodie would know the message had been opened. How would he explain it? He would just say that he mistook her phone for his and had opened the message without realising. He felt like a complete and utter arsehole. He grabbed a piece of paper and a pen and scribbled a note to his wife. *"Sorry babe, was rushing this morning and heard a message beep on the phone, thought it was mine and opened it accidentally, what an idiot!" Love you xxx*

Paranoid and a liar. He grabbed his keys and headed out of the door swearing under his breath as he went.

December 1988

After leaving the solicitor's office, Stella and Roger sat in the car together. He could tell that Stella didn't really want to discuss what had just happened, but he wanted to make sure she was okay. 'Honey, you don't have to go through this alone, I'm here, you know, to read the letter with you, to support you.'

'Why didn't Aunt Gabby say anything to me, Roger, all these years and she never even hinted that there was a letter.'

'I don't know, maybe she did it to protect you, to not hurt you any more than you were hurting already.' There was a long pause. 'I'm scared to open it,' Stella said with a sad look on her face. 'I know, darling, I know.'

'Look, Roger, I know you mean well, and I appreciate all your support and help, but really, please, can we not talk about it at the moment, I just need to get my head straight.' He knew, from her tone, that she was done talking about it and it was best he let things be and left her alone. Stella could be so incredibly vulnerable at times and when she was, he loved her more than ever, but she also had a very hard, impenetrable side to her and when this side emerged, it was best to leave her be. 'Let's go home, Roger, I'm very tired.' They drove home in silence as the rain lashed against the windscreen.

Present Day

Jodie woke up the following morning feeling happy and wide awake ready for the day ahead. She always slept well after lovemaking with Steve and last night had been no exception. After their meal and discussing a weekend away in Paris, one of her favourite destinations, it was inevitable they would end up making love on the sofa. One of her looks and she had Steve right where she wanted him. Even so, he didn't seem himself. 'You sure you're okay,' she had asked several times the previous evening.

'Yeah, babe, I'm fine, really.' Maybe he was secretly pissed off that she wasn't going to the gala dinner with him but if that were the case, he didn't say anything. Steve had left early for work, no change there then. She went into their home gym and did her morning workout. Stretches, crunches, 20 minutes of cardio and finished with a run on the treadmill. She was toned, and there wasn't an ounce of fat on her slim body. She rarely left the house without a workout each day. It was part of her routine. Steve joined her sometimes but, lately, he had been too busy. She showered, dressed in a tailored white suit by her favourite designer which showed off her enviable figure, black heels and black clutch bag. She'd always had good taste when it came to fashion, and today was no exception. She walked to the kitchen and opened the fridge. She always ate breakfast and decided on a slice of toast with honey, healthy and tasty. She finished her toast and put her plate in the sink. She glanced over and saw a note with her name on. It was from Steve telling her he'd accidentally read a text from Rachel as he'd thought it was his phone. 'Silly sod,' she said to herself. For a fleeting moment, she was annoyed, not because she had anything to hide but because she was irritated that he'd read her message knowing it must have been her phone and not his. Still, she had a busy day ahead and was so looking forward to catching up with Rachel. She had so much to tell her. With one final spray of her favourite perfume, she left the house and got into her car.

December 1988

Stella sat in the bath, candles lit, classical music playing in the background. It had been a week since she and Roger had gone to see the solicitor. A week since she had been given the envelope that contained her mother's suicide note. One week. 'Stella, darling, you don't have to read it by yourself if you don't want to, I can be there with you or read it for you, if you like.' Roger, so kind, so caring, so innocently unaware that she was reeling from the revelation that this "note" had only come to surface, now, years after her beloved mother took her own life. 'No, I'm fine, I'm fine, please Roger, just leave me be, okay?'

'Are you sure?'

'Yes, honestly, I'm sure.' She emerged her slim body into the hot, soapy water and looked up at the ceiling. 'Why didn't you tell me, Aunt Gabby?' she whispered to herself. Initially, she was angry with Gabby, angry that she had been denied the chance to read the letter for all these years, but then reasoned with herself that her aunt was protecting her until she was older, it made sense thinking in this way. Her aunt would never have caused her emotional pain for no reason, she knew that deep down. She reached over to the small table beside the bath and picked up the glass of white wine and took a swig. She felt quite relaxed as the effect of the alcohol slid down her throat, into her stomach. The candles flickered in the distance and the sound of the classical music which she loved, washed over her. Roger was out for the evening, a meeting with friends at the Gardeners' Club. It was good to be alone, time to think, time to reflect and time to decide when to open the suicide note that had remained in the drawer on her bedside table for the past week. She stood up, grabbed her towel and stepped out of the bath. After drying herself off, she picked up her glass of wine, walked naked into the bedroom and put on her dressing gown. She lied down on the bed, took a sip of wine, reached over and opened the drawer on her bedside table and took out the white envelope. It was time. She took a deep breath, opened the envelope and began to read.

'My one and only Stells,

I want to start this letter by saying that you are the most important thing in this entire world to me. You are my very soul, my breath, my life, my absolute everything. I don't want you to hate me, whatever you do, don't hate me. I know I'm a coward, too afraid to carry on in this life, too scared to face a future when I can barely face the present.

Stella started to tremble and felt the bile rise in her throat but continued to read.

'For a long time now, I've felt so very afraid and alone. I've not been able to confide in anyone as I don't know how to, all I know is that I won't burden you with the pain I feel inside. I love you too much for that, my baby girl. Having you was the most amazing thing that has ever happened to me, I want you to know that and I am so, so proud of the beautiful young lady you have become. I know I am being selfish, but by setting myself free, I will set you free.

Stella, please don't hate me, please don't let this map the rest of your life. I just can't go on, I'm, (scribbled out words followed which Stella could not understand) *just so very sad and too much of a coward to carry on. But please know this. I will be with you, each and every day, please know that, please don't be scared, don't be afraid, don't be sad. Live your life to the full, do everything you want to do, travel, be crazy, reach for the stars, take chances but most of all, always be who you are! Don't ever stop being my beautiful daughter. Gabby loves you just as much as I do, and I know she will be there for you and take good care of you.*

I'm so sorry, please forgive me.

Love,

Mum xxx

Stella noticed that the words were blurred then realised they were stained with her tears. 'Oh, Mum,' she whispered. She had done it. She had opened the envelope and read the letter addressed to her, the letter that had been in Gabby's possession for so long, the letter that she had given her solicitor to pass on to her niece, her mother's final goodbye. She put her knees to her chest, put the note to her lips and gently kissed it. 'I forgive you, Mum, I forgive you,' she whispered as she slowly rocked back and forth on the bed.

Present Day

Roger put the phone down and smiled to himself. He loved being busy and today was no exception. The doorbell rang and he went to answer it. Eric stood there. 'Hey, buddy, how's it going?'

'Good,' Eric replied.

'Take a look at the plans with me for a second, I think it's just what the Maddison's had in mind, here, take a look.' Eric walked over to the table where Roger had laid out the plans and they were magnificent. 'You've certainly done yourself proud here, my friend,' Eric said. 'I think they'll go for it quite honestly, plus, it will be easy to maintain, which is just what they wanted.'

'You're looking very smart today, Roger, we're only going for lunch,' he chuckled.

'Yes, I know, but it's always good to make an impression, don't you think?' Roger replied, cheerfully. 'Anyway, let's get going, my old friend, places to go and people to see, you know how it is.' They left the house and got into Roger's van and set off for the Maddison's house.

September 1992

It was their fourth wedding anniversary and Roger had quite the surprise for Stella. He just hoped she would see it that way. They'd both been very busy with their work and needed a break, together. No interruptions. He'd booked them a week away in Rome. He'd been there before, with his brother, before he'd met Stella, but she'd not been and had mentioned it was a place she'd love to see. He'd bought her roses, cooked a meal and presented her with the tickets, business class and they were staying in a five-star hotel in the centre of the city.

'Wow, Roger, this is wonderful,' she'd said when he'd presented her with the tickets. 'Rome, I've always wanted to go there!' She'd kissed him on the lips and hugged him tightly. 'I know, that's why I thought it would be good for us, you know, get away, we've both been so busy lately and we could both do with the break and what better time than our anniversary,' he'd exclaimed excitedly.

'Thank you, darling, it's so thoughtful of you. It really is,' Stella had replied. He was happy that she had reacted this way and the following weekend, they jetted off for Rome. It was just the tonic they both needed. They visited all the historical places of interest. They went to see The Spanish Steps, The Coliseum and the Trevi Fountain. 'Come on, let's make a wish,' Roger had declared and they both closed their eyes and tossed a coin into the water. It was like when they had first met. They enjoyed lovemaking in the big, king-sized bed, walked hand in hand around the city, ate pasta and pizza every day and slept until late morning and then ate breakfast in bed. It was just like the old days and Roger could not have been happier. 'Thank you, Roger, this is just wonderful, just what we needed,' Stella said to him. He smiled at her and said, 'I love you, Stella Sinclair-Matthews,' and hugged her closely. Stella rarely gave compliments and it was good to see her in such a good mood. On their fourth day of the holiday, Roger ventured out early in the morning to buy Stella the small, heart-shaped necklace he'd seen in the window of small jewellers a couple of streets away and left Stella sleeping. The previous evening had been wonderful. They'd been to a very expensive restaurant on the outskirts of the city, and enjoyed authentic Italian cuisine, two bottles of expensive white wine and a brandy each, after dessert. They'd laughed, talked about things and Roger had not seen Stella this relaxed in a long time. She was being affectionate and loving and as soon as they'd got back to their hotel, they'd fallen on the bed and made love into the early hours. Roger was so happy. He felt he had the Stella back that he'd married. He bought the necklace and the lady in the shop had wrapped it up in its small box with gold, vibrant paper. He left the shop and was heading back to the hotel when he heard someone call his name. 'Roger!' He turned around and facing him was Grace, his ex-girlfriend. It took him a couple of seconds to register, but it was Grace. 'Oh my God,' she said, 'I can't believe it, fancy seeing you here.' She was a lot heavier than he'd remembered and her hair was much shorter. 'Grace, blimey. How are you?' It was a bit of a shock seeing her after all these years.

'Wow, Roger it's so good to see you, I'm good, I'm here with my husband, Phil. He's here on business and it's a little break from the rat race.'

'I'm here with my wife, Stella.' Was it just his imagination, or did he notice a flicker of disappointment in Grace's face? 'Oh, so you're married too?' Grace asked.

'Yes, four years now, we live in Cornwall.'

'Do you have time for a coffee?' Grace asked him. 'Phil's at a business meeting and it would be great to catch up with you.' She was smiling at him. He thought about it for a second and said, 'Yes, sure, there's a little place down the road, we could go there.' As they sat together, he thought back to the last time he'd seen her. It was an image he'd never forget, writhing with Teddy, their naked bodies as one. It was a long time ago now but seeing her brought it back to him. 'Roger, I know a lot of time has passed, and we've both moved on.' She looked uncomfortable, and he wasn't sure he wanted her to carry on, so he stopped her mid-sentence.

'Grace, let's not go over all of that, okay, I mean, I'm very happy now, my wife's amazing, I've got a great life and I'm sure you do too. We were young and stupid back then, really, it doesn't matter anymore.'

'No, Roger, it does matter, it matters to me. I know I hurt you and believe me when I say I've had to live with that, me and Teddy. It meant nothing, really.' Roger ignored her and started to regret coming to the café with her for coffee. 'Listen, Grace, I have to go, it was great to see you again and—' she cut him off. 'Roger, please. There's something I have to tell you.' Roger didn't like her tone, he felt uncomfortable, but Grace carried on. 'When you left that day, you know, when you walked out, well, I tried to call you so many times and you wouldn't take my calls.' Roger remained silent. 'Well, boy, I really don't know how to say this, but, well…' she hesitated, 'I was pregnant, Roger, pregnant with your baby.' Roger stared at her and could feel his heart beating faster and faster. 'Pregnant?' was all he could say. 'Yes, I, I only found out after you'd moved and didn't know how to reach you.'

'Shit, shit,' Roger stammered. Grace went on, 'I was so confused and scared. I felt so alone and, and…' she stammered.

'What?' Roger managed to say.

'I had an abortion, Roger,' Grace blurted out. She was looking at him now, trying to read his face, searching for a clue as to what he was thinking. 'Was it mine?' Roger asked coldly. 'I mean you were fucking Teddy, so was it mine?' The venom in his voice scared Grace and she got up from the table. 'I'm sorry, Roger, I just, well, I just thought you should know, I didn't tell you to hurt you, I just thought you had a right to know, after all, the chance of bumping into you like this and all, well, I thought it was the right thing to do.'

'Grace,' he too got up and looked at her ugly, fat and bloated face, 'Grace, if meeting you unexpectedly here, in Rome, has shown me one thing it's this.' He was not the Roger she had remembered, the caring, loving, funny young guy who would tell her how beautiful she was. His face was contorted with rage. 'It has shown me that I had a lucky escape from a conniving, twisted, nasty evil bitch, so I want to thank you, Grace.' He turned and left her standing there and walked out of the café. He was so angry his heart was still beating fast. He had met her by chance after all these years and she had dropped this bombshell. He fastened his pace towards the hotel where his beautiful wife Stella lay sleeping in their bed. She, the slut, had aborted his baby. He would have been a dad. Grace had taken away that chance, the bitch. He could not hold back the tears any longer. He entered a side street, slid down the wall and began to sob his heart out. After what seemed like an eternity, he composed himself and headed back to the hotel.

'Hi, darling.' Stella was already up and putting on her makeup in the bathroom. 'Hi, honey, did you sleep okay? he said.

'Sure did, have a bit of a thick head though, that wine was lovely,' Stella chuckled. For the rest of the holiday, Roger tried to act as normal as possible, even though his wife asked him if he was okay many times as he seemed a little quiet. 'Yes, darling, I'm just a little tired and it's back to work next week!' he said, even convincing himself. He had always been very open with Stella and didn't hide anything from her. Although she may have been different from him and found it hard to show her emotions, he just could not share with her what he had discovered. Could not tell her that he'd, by pure chance, bumped into his ex-girlfriend and she'd dropped the bombshell that she'd aborted his baby. It was his secret and it would stay that way.

Present Day

Steve had arrived at the office before anyone else, but it was still too early to call Stella, or was it? Yes, he would do it after his first meeting of the morning. In fact, he could arrange to meet her, and she could give back the information he had passed on the day before, including Jodie's photo. He would pay her for her time and trouble and be on his way. After his first meeting of the day, Steve went into his office and dialled Stella's number. 'Hi, Stella, this is Steve, Steve Abbott. I'm sorry to bother you but...' he hesitated, 'listen, I've made a mistake and don't want to you go ahead with what we discussed yesterday, please can you call me as soon as you get this message, okay, thanks.' The afternoon sunlight was starting to disappear behind the clouds and the sky looked quite spectacular. Stella made sure she followed Jodie at a safe distance and found herself, about an hour later, on a steep, coastal road which led to beautiful, yet quaint, very expensive houses high up in the vibrant, green hills overlooking the ocean below. A taxi passed her on the other side of the road going way too fast, 'Bloody idiot!' she mumbled under her breath. The way some people drive, honestly. Jodie was a fast driver, but Stella still managed to follow her at a safe distance. She could feel the anticipation in the pit of her stomach that she was onto something as according to the time and day, Jodie should be at the gym. Steve had told her she always did a yoga class at this time every Tuesday. There was no way Jodie planned on doing yoga today, Stella thought. They were miles away from the gym and the town by now. Yes, Jodie definitely took excellent care of herself. There was no doubt about that, but she would not be attending a yoga class tonight. 'Shit!' Steve said angrily. It had been hours since he had left Stella a message. Why had she not called him back? He dialled her number and once again, it went straight to voicemail. He hung up, feeling pissed off. 'Shit, just bloody pick up the phone, woman!' he muttered angrily. As they ascended the winding road, Stella remained a safe distance behind. Jodie slowed down and drove onto a gravelled driveway outside a beautiful house, surrounded by big, robust trees. Stella could see perfectly from where she had parked, and Jodie turned off her engine and got out of her car. She was smiling to herself with a spring in her step that Stella had seen so many times before. Whereas the whole day had been rather normal and mundane, something told Stella this was all about to change. *Something's not right here, and I pray to God, it's not what my gut instinct is telling me*, Stella thought to herself. Boy, she was so damn good at her job. She was worth every penny of what some would say was a very hefty fee. But she always got results, even if those results ending up breaking hearts and families. Stella got out of her car and followed Jodie without being seen, or of course, heard. By now it was dusk, which was a good thing. With one last flick of her long, chestnut hair, Jodie approached the front door, turned the key, entered the house and closed the door behind her. Stella, expensive camera at the ready, got as close as she could to the nearest window and saw the flickering of candles in what seemed to be, one of the bedrooms. She couldn't see Jodie or anyone else for that matter but was sure that the photographic evidence which would break Steve's heart and no doubt possibly end his marriage would come her way at any moment. She could feel the excitement running through her veins, as she had so many times before. And then she saw Jodie enter the bedroom, holding the hand of a man she had seen so many times before, a man who was laughing, pulling Jodie close to him, running his hands through her long, beautiful hair, kissing her passionately on the mouth as Jodie responded in earnest. It was Roger, her Roger, her husband. Roger and Jodie were staring at each other like young lovers as they started undressing each other. The sharp, stabbing pain across Stella's chest was so sudden and so unbearable that she dropped her camera and with it, fell to the floor in agony. This was Stella's husband. Stella's shy, boring, predictable, introverted husband, Roger. Just before Stella died, she realised with tears streaming down her face, that she had never, in ten years of marriage, told Roger just how much she loved him.

THE END

CPSIA information can be obtained
at www.ICGtesting.com
Printed in the USA
BVHW090834100919
558042BV00017B/342/P